Us in the Flesh

SEBASTIAN BERNINZONI

To my parents and all kinds of love.

Lily Something

Tell me one thing you tell someone before they die
    and I'll lay haunted by
    you did everything right
    upside
    bright side
    down
    flower
    tumbling and wind bound
    forgotten forever.

Anabelle Orange (Death and Dying)

Delicately unwraps
  rough skin
  from paper brown bag
  flat peel squared
  bright orange flesh
  calloused guitar hands
  raise a slice to her mouth
  handkerchief top
  sweet
  dripping
  almost sticky breeze
  all humid in the northeast
  separates strands of hair
  to hang around
  and leave olive sleeves rolled up
  close to her
  keeping secret
  quiet
  and most importantly
  cool
  while I sit here
  and keep
  film
  from someone I hate.

Up the staircase and down the hallway.

Stems

Days are ticking by
      probably the most left object on the ground.
      I like how we share toothpaste even though I have my own.
      It's because yours is sweeter and you laugh when I tell you
      about boys on benches
      or in briefs,
      saying goodbye
      for closure
      or hope of another life.
      He will keep telling me I smell like bug spray
      even when I catch fireflies to show you how delicate
      a good harmony would do
      to a melody I'm not sure is mine.

The hanging of laundry- surprisingly graceful.

Lichen (Confronting Grammar)

There is paper in my lunch
    and so I'll write about trash.
    He taught me how to pronounce it and sat
    in green grass Arizona fields
    only when I close my eyes
    and think about my past
    plus the way to peel ~~an orange~~ grapefruit
    because that's what I can't eat
    Many bitter poison
    especially to so many *here*.
    How manly
    but he claims is a lovely treat.
    So get up
    and do what she said
    do what you did in July.

Close-up of dip dye scarf making.

Custodial Autonomy

It's 10 PM and only home has my bedtime
 and my room is a space where shadows aren't eerie
 but playlist pictures.

 Navy blue waffle blanket comes with me
 while the high-pitched hum of my electric life
 lives on
 piecing together like Sunny Saturday.

 and when I stop and think,
 staring at Mediterranean textured ceilings,
 that anyone can do anything in the dark:

 I feel a little less weird
 and a lot less normal.

Patience at a dinner party.

Normally Rejection Can Scare Off Things Like Birds:

Stay sunny so the dirt dries out to make it easier on my shoes and back.

    I can see my reflection at the bottom of the sink
    basin
    as I brush my teeth

    For the first time I see
    headboard to bedframe
    2 songs
    time
    top bunk
    around 6 minutes
    and the rainboots are stiff
    out of rain, in cabins.
    And I'll never think of that again
    And how when I ask how things are
    And you say fine
    I think of lightning camera flash.

    We cant play sports
    but we are awfully good at kicking rocks
    on hiking dirt roads
    to hit the backs of coupled shoes.

Water folds

tree shimmer shadows

I'll get to the point.

Summer 2019. Best then, worst now.

Stars: Take Me On

I remember walking up to 81st Street to see the East River
    I didn't know you then
    We walk a different river miles north now
    Hudson confusion
    proving water does flow in the right direction.
    She says were are losing our minds
    but you weren't there.
    Let me show you what I see in the sky
    because city kid in you keeps it bright
    light pollution.
    I can't stand to look to my right and see ~~Maui~~
    because everything is more starry where you met me.
    Track honeycomb,
    pavements,
    and invasive
    planted grass in between.

Anderson Writes Every Other Photo Poem:

I say meet me at the ballroom

    bring a camera

    one that can record and capture

    light will enter the lens and time will stop.

    Memory eternal,

    but it plays better in my head.

    Terrifying actually.

    Reveals truths

    application

    covers lies

    to live on

    almost indestructible

    like how everyone forgets diamond is carbon

    and the devil is temptation.

Sonnet-Bound Huntington Bay

Clean beachy slides grip the pavement of Taylor Street on Huntington Bay.

We sit on warped rocky docks. Sets of feet, lined up, soles grazing the sunset water.

Salty air through curly hair.

Pass the sweaty leather flask with

bathroom-poured Jameson, please.

The fleeting sunlight casts oil spill on surface tension science.

Count your days I say

to a group I love more than late-night highway

but will never really know me anyway.

Cheers.

Tricks

I haven't seen you in so long
    and my heart skips beats
    leaving blood on sad girl's face
    watery eyes and believe me when I say
    Los Angeles suits me best
    leave you
    it all
    behind
    behind.

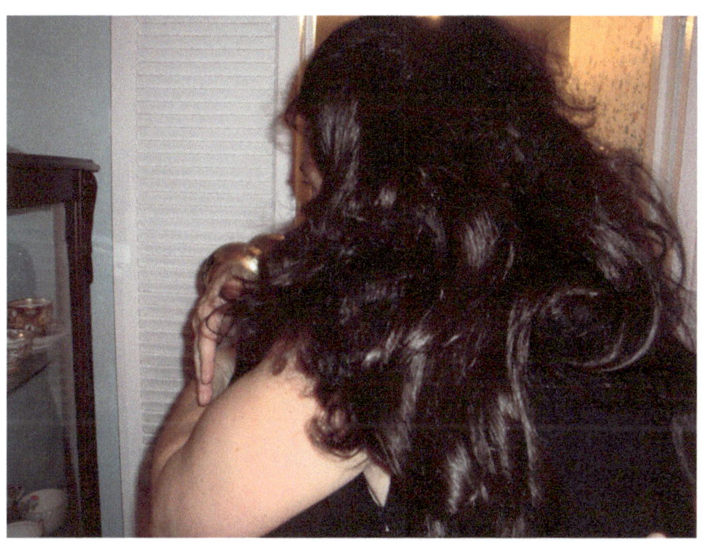

Fever?

Someone cleans the kitchen

   and so I know I'm not alone

   mostly because cats lie in moonlight streetlights.

   Cigar smoke stings my eyes while I eat a late dinner.

   The important are sleeping

   but the real are here

   again reminded, stinging.

   When I finished a read,

   tragedy,

   I thought of a window

   and knew of a mirror.

   As I am set on upside-down letters

   maybe words

   dropping hobbies

   for a sickness

   that wants its way

   typecase.

Nighttime alleyway "somewhere in northern Italy".

I Love It Here

Here is where I sunbathe

    and here is where paint chips lie pretty

    Here is where windows swing open

    and here is where cicadas buzz

    Here is where the sunset drives

    and here is where more orange is warmth than ever before

    Here is where the air is sweeter

    and here is where I don't say bye.

    And I love it there

    but here

    that's where I can sigh.

Street corner in Monterosso.

It's Called Switching Letters and Kidnapping

You could be anywhere
even in your homeroom
and I'll still see you
under the hazy canopy
orange sunlit room with a curly, wooden,
rustic framework,
wasting time.
We got the best photo taken there-
out the window and down the pavilion.
Shut up
die laughing
wakeup call.
You made a house feel like home
with you
even if it was for only two weeks,
the view was forever

Are your bags packed?

Rivera and My Apocalypse

The light sunburn on my back meets linen sheets
    and the abundance of sea glass on the coasts between
    you and me.
    Hazy, like me guessing,
    and abrasive like your jokes.
    Nice to step on
    and nicer to hang up
    on
    punishment in the glass case.

    And unlike these doctors, I can't tell how you're feeling.
    I'll go home and even though I'm closer to you,
    only there,
    keeps me alive-
    deep in books and learning
    but is barely a street sign to you.

"Rivera"

"Apocalypse"

Structural Problems Facing North

Tell me and it will be my pleasure
    to discover a new town,
    the one where you are from.
    Just like that,
    smashing escape
    to front seat smiles,
    ironic construction,
    and my bracelet on your wrist,
    not forgetting yours on mine.
    That's trust
    like no other.
    Even when across the country
    and we said goodbye twice.
    A summation of tears that morning and quarter-night.
    So months later,
    three hours into the future,
    I still can't go to Kingston for two more reasons-
    the same reasons that
    we exchange information through windows
    and synchronize our footsteps.
    The ultimate
    psychiatric fuck.

Water in the Worst Way

Like,
Fast charge
long line
bureaucracy crimes.
So anyways,
flight or
fight or
freeze.
I guess,
consumption
undoubtedly equitable
according to
them but
he does
not like
us and
them says
borderline them.
Yeah.

I don't think you get it. Yet.

The metro in everywhere but a metropolis.

Windows down

Sunflower seed rolls in my mouth,
    rough on my tongue.
    I can't remember what worried me at nine
    but I'm sure it was important enough to ruin a perfectly good
night.
    And a perfectly good place.
    All the shows I watched with my parents
    heavy napping in a hammock
    and my secret New years' resolution
    is all a part of me.
    Most of everything like this can make me smile
    every now and then.
    It's mostly ice cream cake on a vista,
    Fort Lauderdale secrets,
    and specific but also incredibly prevalent
    antique bathroom tile
    that slip on my dreams
    sometimes,
    when others
    I just
    envision a place I've never gone
    never will go
    or can.

Professional banker at work.

You Made That Word Up

I hear the fan
   and the old TV turn on
   in my room
   and at memory home
   but no one else hears.
   Like screaming from my tears-
   no fear
   or cares.

...

Subsist

I'm soaking wet and all I know is Adriatic aquatics.

How do you keep a straight face—

all that language wrapped up

just for guests.

I know how deep the water is

because you told me in meaningless meters.

Sleeping on the steps of the basilica-

cicadas sonic,

in and out.

I feel like I'm drowning even when the water just splashed my
face.

My Star of David rests above where my white dress shirt
closes.

And the sea salt on your chest,

humana o gentes?

Smile wide

and taste the sea.

Teach me to drive and windward side

star bound and tied up

left me by metal handlebars.

My hands were healed

and now they're peeling.

Thank you

because I don't know how to say

thank you

so,

very

much.

Sunset on the Ligurian Sea

Mountain high town
  with only one,
  a long way,
  down.
  Windy roads that make me worried-
  phone lines and uncontrolled radio.
  Everything is fine
  and by this time of day,
  most of my friends are awake.
  Signs of a café
  and climbing vines
  because wolves, I am told
  are magical-
  almost biographical.
  I can't tell what's different here but it might be the water
  because I see sailboats where I'm from.
  Still, the ocean is loved by me
  and more than I.
  Black backpack and matching Levi's
  just like us.
  And it's only thirty-eight miles
  but it will take longer than expected
  for sure.

What Did I Do July?

I remember the apricots I saw a few miles down the road.

    Heading south left me at July 24

your house

and only the youngest on the fridge.

Do you feel like family?

Because your teen sister I knew

driving

feels foreign.

It's cold here but the night air carries warmth

almost like it's coming from somewhere sunny.

Not better,

just brighter.

Cardinal direction

frying oil

long flights

last year's music.

I forgot how much I like spending time with you.

Stay here

but not the night.

Fire Island, NY

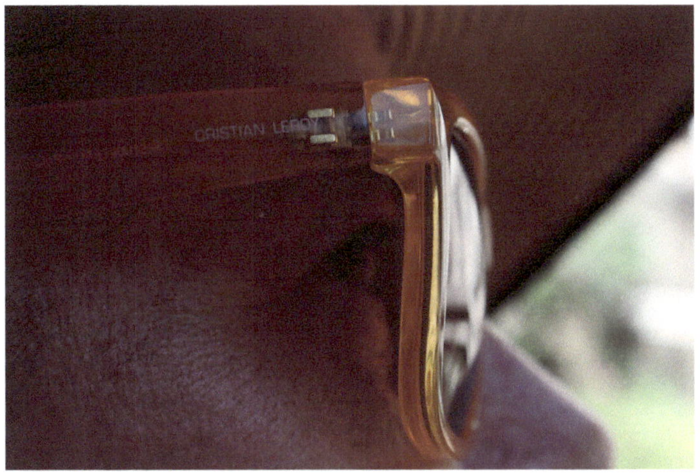

Eden Okay

I want to spend my warm summer nights with you,
 last bits of glistening daylight, let us leave on a rose-red canoe
in a lake of which we couldn't care for a name.
 Paddling out to the middle,
 just for us to stop and look at the scenery
 that is each other.
 I'll cook dinner on linoleum stovetops and expect a tip-toed
kiss on the cheek every night, a few minutes prior to its comple-
tion.
 Let us watch movies till midnight,
 get sick off popcorn,
 and head off to bed,
 our fingers, still sticky with butter.
 Entangled in sheets and gripped covers
 with enough wrinkles to be a vast choppy ocean.

With your hand and a call of mine, drag me to the seashore
 where we will find
 sand on soles
 wet drips of purple shell
 and the look on others' faces when we pose for nothing
 and everything
 but a kiss.

Bravery I

Bravery II

Bravery III

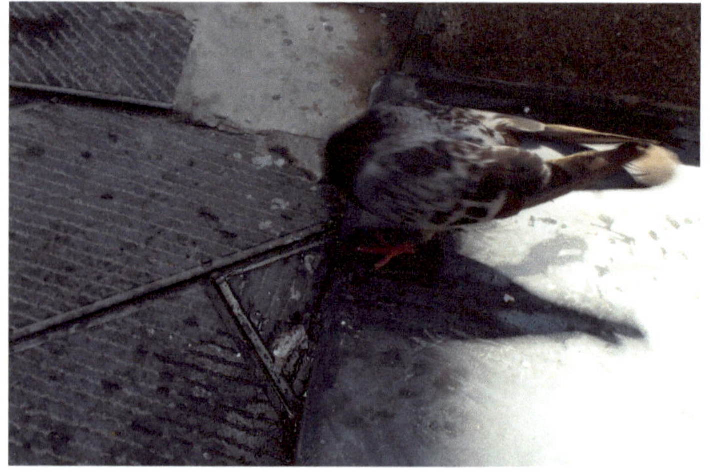

Bravery IV

Interstate

How beautiful a serene escape
    walking towards the rainy side of town
    when last night I had the darkest light reflect my face.
    And all I could do is stare at my fingers interlaced
    holding myself through it.
    Crack and feel,
    watching the drapes.

"Villa"

Tablespoon

Last time I saw you was about half a year ago and you stole from the party supplies store for almost no reason. You strolled out and gripped the party favor in your hands.

Kinda like you almost hated it for making it so easy.

With kneaded air bubbles and new warmth, it became tough, rejecting you

once again

once again

both of your hands reach into your goose feather puffer jacket

and take out the shell. You slide the mess inside the hard plastic case and throw it to the ground.

Now, I ask you why

and you say

I wouldn't want anyone to get anything on their shoes.

And now,

apathy will kill us all, but it really killed you.

Try Looking Up at 42nd Street

Take it in.

I've been here somewhat recently.

A week before Christmas and the snow was a top sheet.

Try listening for the lights this time of year. You can almost hear a faint buzz that mimics bees on countryside warm months.

Stars and body heat.

Candlelight, nuclear fusion, and Paul Helleu.

Only a very specific part of the city is home to me.

It might be the part you're in:

a part

and somewhere I've never seen before.

Advantage

The necklace clasp in the front woke me up from the strangest
dream.

    I'm also only tending to notice the moon after dawn
    on a walk down my driveway
    and I'll try to take a picture
    cause' my memory's shit and if I don't
    it never happened
    and so let me know
    if making something out of nothing
    is just one thing my brain does
    or its the work of a traitor
    philosopher
    dealer
    influencer
    and maybe or rhetorician
    because I missed the train
    lept in
      procrastinated-
      by the way is

herability when no one remembers your birth-

And do I listen just to

get the advantage?

"IMG_1000.jpg"

Grateful Something

Rocks dig into my knees
   Bending down
   Bending Tree.
   Thank god
   but I don't know what to say
   because what if he hates me.
   That's what people tell me.
   And what if the Mayans were right?
   The world ended in 2012.
   When I place my compulsions in the fire,
   burning my intentions,
   and stopping myself from falling ill
   because god loves everyone
   except for the sick.

Us in the Flesh (Poem)

It's been me and you
   for however long I want it to
   and we've seen diner paintings
   and stirred their coffee
   like old friends waiting for their time apart
   to synchronize, feeling the same old beestings.
   Plastic board game pieces
   and clicks of pens
   might be American visas
   to those by the seashore
   like me and maybe you.
   It's always us, the rest
   and I can touch you-
   hold your hand.
   Definitely, not nearly, a mirage.
   So,
   and forever I hope,
   it's us
   in the flesh.

Stars on arms
drawn with ink
lie more black
than bright white
in the real night sky
and while the incessant clock ticks
precision
front row seat
feels like fire under me
now lazy
and to be gifted
is just a memory.

Advantage

The necklace clasp in the front woke me up from the strangest dream.

    I'm also only tending to notice the moon after dawn

on a walk down my driveway

and I'll try to take a picture

cause' my memory's shit and if I don't

it never happened

and so let me know

if making something out of nothing

is just one thing my brain does

or its the work of a traitor

philosopher

dealer

influencer

and maybe or rhetorician

because I missed the train

slept in

and procrastinated-

which by the way is

so

so

human.

    So, what is vulnerability when no one remembers your birthday?

And do I listen just to

get the advantage?

"IMG_1000.jpg"